DEBORAH

A MODERN TALE OF LOVE AND LEADERSHIP

WOMEN OF THE BIBLE FICTION
BOOK 5

KAYLA LOWE

Want a free book? Sign up to my newsletter to get my award-winning book for free! www.authorkaylalowe.com

MORE OF MY BOOKS

<u>Series</u>

<u>Charms of the Chaste Court</u>

A Courtship in Covent Garden
Whispers in Westminster
Romance in Regent's Park
Serenade on Strand Street
Treasure in Tower Bridge

<u>Sweet Honey by the Sea</u>

<u>The Beekeeper's Secret (Book 1)</u>
<u>A Royal Honeycomb (Book 2)</u>
<u>Bees in Blossom (Book 3)</u>
<u>Honeyed Kisses (Book 4)</u>
<u>Blooming Forever (Book 5)</u>

<u>Strawberry Beach Series</u>

<u>Beachside Lessons (Book 1)</u>
<u>Beachside Lessons (Book 2)</u>
<u>Beachside Lessons (Book 3)</u>

Panama City Beach Series

Sun-Kissed Secrets (Book 1)
Sun-Kissed Secrets (Book 2)
Sun-Kissed Secrets (Book 3)

The Tainted Love Saga

Of Love and Deception (Book 1)
Of Love and Family (Book 2)
Of Love and Violence (Book 3)
Of Love and Abuse(Book 4)
Of Love and Crime (Book 5)
Of Love and Addiction (Book 6)
Of Love and Redemption (Book 7)

Standalones

Maiden's Blush

Poetry

Phantom Poetry
Lost and Found

CHAPTER 1

The stage lights illuminated Deborah's face as she stepped up to the podium, her blue eyes scanning the audience of business leaders and professionals gathered before her. She took a deep breath, the weight of her message settling on her shoulders like a mantle of responsibility.

"Integrity," she began, her voice clear and commanding, "is the cornerstone upon which we must build our businesses, our communities, and our lives."

Deborah's words hung in the air, demanding attention and introspection from all who listened. She spoke of the temptations that come with power and success, the easy paths of compromise and corruption that could lead even the most principled astray. Yet, she reminded them, it was in these moments of choice that true character was forged.

As she spoke, memories of her own battles against unethical practices flashed through her mind—the long nights spent pouring over financial reports, the tense boardroom confrontations, the whispered threats from those who preferred the status quo. Each challenge had tested her resolve, but she had emerged stronger, more committed to her values than ever before.

"We are the guardians of our own integrity," Deborah said, her gaze sweeping the room. "It is a responsibility we cannot abdicate, a duty we owe to ourselves and to those who depend on us."

She painted a vision of a business world where honesty and fairness were not just platitudes but guiding principles, where success was measured not just in profits but in the positive impact made on lives and communities. It was a world she had fought for all her life and would continue to fight for, no matter the cost.

As her speech drew to a close, Deborah's voice grew softer, more reflective. "In the end," she said, "we will be judged not by our titles or our bank accounts, but by the content of our character. Let us strive every day to be leaders of integrity, in our businesses and in our lives."

The audience rose to their feet in a standing ovation as she stepped back from the podium, but Deborah barely noticed the applause. Her mind was already turning to the battles ahead, the injustices that still needed to be righted. She knew her work was far from over, but with conviction burning in her heart, she was ready to face whatever challenges lay ahead. For in the fight for integrity, there could be no retreat, no surrender - only the unwavering determination to do what was right, no matter the odds.

Boarded-up windows and "For Lease" signs adorned the once-vibrant storefronts along Main Street, a testament to the conglomerate's suffocating grip on the city's economy. The few pedestrians who braved the sidewalks moved with a sense of dejection, their shoulders slumped under the weight of an uncertain future. In the distance, the gleaming tower of the conglomerate's headquarters loomed like a modern-day citadel, casting a long shadow over the struggling neighborhood.

Deborah navigated her car through the potholed streets, her heart heavy as she witnessed the decay firsthand. The speech she had given at the conference seemed a distant memory now, her words of integrity and fairness ringing hollow in the face of such blatant exploitation. She tightened her grip on the steering wheel, a silent vow to herself that she would not let this injustice stand.

As she turned the corner, Deborah's eyes widened at the sight before her. A crowd had gathered outside the gates of a factory, their signs and chants demanding fair wages and job security. Police officers in riot gear formed a barricade, their batons at the ready. The tension in the air was palpable, a powder keg waiting for a spark.

Deborah pulled to the curb, her mind racing. She knew the factory well—it had been a pillar of the community for generations, providing stable employment for hundreds of families. Now, it seemed, it had fallen victim to the conglomerate's insatiable appetite for profit.

A man broke from the crowd, his face etched with desperation. "Please, Ms. Lawson," he pleaded, recognizing her from the news. "You have to help us. They're shutting down the factory, laying off everyone. We don't know what we're going to do."

Deborah's heart clenched at the raw emotion in his voice. She knew all too well the pain of losing one's livelihood, the fear of not being able to provide for one's family. In that moment, the path before her crystallized with a clarity that took her breath away.

"I will help you," she said, her voice steady with resolve. "I don't know how yet, but I promise you, I will do everything in my power to make this right."

The man's eyes glistened with unshed tears as he nodded his thanks. Deborah watched as he rejoined the crowd, their chants taking on a new fervor in the face of her pledge.

As she drove away, Deborah's mind churned with the enormity of the task before her. Taking on the conglomerate would be no easy feat—they had money, power, and influence on their side. But she had something more—the unshakeable conviction that what they were doing was wrong, and the determination to see justice served.

In the rearview mirror, the factory faded from view, but its image remained seared in Deborah's mind—a symbol of all that had been lost, and all that she would fight to reclaim. The road ahead would be long and fraught with challenges, but she knew in her heart that it was a journey she had to take. For the sake of the city she loved, and for the people who called it home, she would not rest until integrity and fairness reigned once more.

Deborah arrived at her office, her mind still reeling from the encounter with the community leaders. She sat at her desk, staring blankly at the reports and spreadsheets that awaited her attention. The numbers blurred together, losing meaning in the face of the real-life struggles she had just witnessed.

She leaned back in her chair, closing her eyes as she tried to process the weight of the responsibility now resting on her shoulders. The conglomerate's actions were not just unethical—they were causing tangible harm to the very fabric of the city. Families were being torn apart, livelihoods destroyed, and dreams shattered.

A knock at the door jolted her from her thoughts. "Come in," she called, straightening in her seat.

Her assistant, Lydia, poked her head into the

room. "Sorry to disturb you, Ms. Lawson, but there's a journalist here to see you. Says he has some information about the conglomerate that you might find interesting."

Deborah's pulse quickened. "Send him in."

A moment later, a man in his early thirties entered the office, a leather satchel slung over his shoulder. "Ms. Lawson, thank you for seeing me on such short notice. I'm Ben Fisher, with the City Chronicle."

She shook his hand, studying him closely. There was an intensity in his gaze that suggested he was more than just another reporter chasing a headline. "What can I do for you, Mr. Fisher?"

He reached into his bag, pulling out a stack of documents. "I've been investigating the conglomerate for months now, and I've uncovered some disturbing information. Bribery, corruption, environmental violations—it goes deep."

Deborah's eyes widened as she flipped through the pages, her heart sinking with each damning revelation. "This is...incredibly compelling evidence. With this, we might actually have a chance of bringing them to justice."

Ben nodded, a grim smile on his face. "I thought you might say that. I've heard about your reputation, Ms. Lawson. If anyone can take on this fight, it's you."

She met his gaze, a newfound sense of purpose crystallizing within her. "Thank you, Mr. Fisher. I promise you, I will not let this information go to waste. The conglomerate's days of operating with impunity are numbered."

As Ben left her office, Deborah felt a flicker of hope amidst the daunting challenge ahead. The road would be long and the opposition fierce, but armed with the truth and the support of those who believed in her, she knew that victory was possible. All that remained was to take that first step, and trust that God would guide her path.

\

CHAPTER 2

The fluorescent lights buzzed overhead as Deborah leaned forward, her fingers steepled, observing the two men seated across from her. Tension crackled in the air, their faces taut with barely restrained anger. She took a slow, measured breath, gathering her thoughts before breaking the heavy silence.

"Gentlemen," Deborah began, her voice even and calm, "I understand the gravity of this situation. But let us remember that we are all striving for the same goal—the betterment of our city and its people."

The older man, a seasoned executive with a reputation for ruthlessness, scoffed. "Pretty words, Ms. Lawson, but they won't solve the very real problems we're facing. This deal is critical for our company's survival."

His younger counterpart, an up-and-coming entrepreneur, interjected, "At what cost? Your so-called 'deal' will destroy everything I've worked for!"

Deborah held up a hand, silencing them both. She fixed each man with her piercing gaze, seeing beyond their blustering facades to the fear and desperation beneath. How many times had she sat in this very chair, mediating conflicts born of greed and pride? Yet, she never lost sight of the human element, the fragile hopes and dreams that hung in the balance.

"I hear your concerns," she said, choosing her words with care. "But I also see an opportunity here – a chance for collaboration rather than competition. Imagine what we could achieve if we pooled our resources and worked together towards a common purpose."

The men exchanged skeptical glances, but Deborah pressed on, her conviction growing with each word. "This city has always been a beacon of innovation and progress. Let us not allow short-sighted self-interest to dim that light. We have the power to create something extraordinary here, something that will benefit generations to come."

As she spoke, Deborah felt a familiar stirring in her soul – a quiet certainty that this was her calling, her purpose. She had been blessed with a gift for leadership, for seeing the potential in others and drawing it out. And now, more than ever, her city needed that gift.

The conversation shifted, tentatively at first, then with growing momentum as Deborah guided the men towards common ground. She knew it was only a small victory in the grand scheme of things, but it gave her hope. With faith and perseverance, she believed they could overcome any obstacle, no matter how daunting.

As the meeting drew to a close and the men departed, shaking hands with newfound respect, Deborah allowed herself a moment of quiet reflection. The path ahead would be difficult, fraught with challenges and setbacks. But she was ready to face them head-on, armed with the unwavering conviction that she was exactly where she was meant to be.

Deborah strode into the small, sparsely decorated office, her eyes immediately drawn to the man seated behind the desk. Barak Thompson, the newly elected city councilman, looked up from a stack of papers, his expression a mix of surprise and trepidation.

"Councilman Thompson," Deborah greeted him, extending a hand. "Thank you for making time to see me."

Barak rose to his feet, shaking her hand with a tentative smile. "Of course, Ms. Lawson. What can I do for you?"

Deborah settled into the chair opposite him, her gaze direct and unwavering. "I'll get straight to the point. I'm here because I believe our city is at a crossroads, and I need your help to ensure we choose the right path."

Barak leaned back in his chair, a furrow appearing between his brows. "I'm not sure I understand. What exactly are you proposing?"

"A coalition," Deborah replied, her voice ringing with conviction. "A united front against the corruption and greed that threaten to destroy everything we hold dear. I know you share my commitment to justice and integrity, Councilman. Together, we can make a real difference."

Barak's eyes widened, and he shook his head slowly. "Ms. Lawson, I appreciate your faith in me, but I'm just one man. What can I possibly do against such powerful forces?"

Deborah leaned forward, her expression softening. "You underestimate yourself, Councilman. I've seen the way you champion the needs of your constituents, the passion with which you fight for what's right. You have a voice that people listen to, a platform that can inspire real change."

Barak looked down at his hands, doubt etched in every line of his face. The weight of responsibility settled heavily on his shoulders, and for a moment, he felt the old familiar tug of uncertainty, the whispered fears that he wasn't enough, that he would inevitably let everyone down.

But as he met Deborah's steady gaze, he saw something else there too—a flicker of understanding, of shared purpose. She believed in him, not just as a politician, but as a person, someone with the courage and conviction to stand up for what was right, no matter the cost.

"I don't know if I'm ready for this," he admitted, his voice barely above a whisper. "The thought of taking on such powerful enemies...it's daunting."

Deborah reached across the desk, her hand

coming to rest lightly on his arm. "I know it's frightening," she said softly. "But we cannot let fear dictate our actions. This city needs us, Barak. It needs our strength, our integrity, our unwavering commitment to justice. Together, we can be a force for change, a beacon of hope in these troubled times."

Barak took a deep breath, feeling something shift inside him, a flicker of courage kindling to life. He thought of all the people counting on him, the lives that hung in the balance. And he knew, with sudden, piercing clarity, that he could not turn his back on them, no matter how daunting the road ahead might be.

"Alright," he said at last, meeting Deborah's eyes with a newfound resolve. "I'm in. Let's do this together."

Deborah smiled, a warm, genuine smile that lit up her face. "Thank you, Barak," she said simply. "I knew I could count on you."

And as they shook hands once more, sealing their alliance with a shared look of determination, Deborah felt a surge of hope, a quiet certainty that they were on the right path. The road ahead would be long and difficult, but with faith and persever-ance, she knew they would prevail. For the sake of their city, for the sake of all those who called it home, failure was simply not an option.

Deborah sat alone in the stillness of her living room, the weight of the city's struggles bearing down upon her shoulders. Through the large bay window, the sprawling metropolis stretched out before her, its towering skyscrapers and winding streets painted in the fading hues of dusk. She watched as the sun dipped below the horizon, casting long shadows across the urban landscape, a poignant reflection of the darkness that threatened to engulf the very soul of the city she called home.

With a heavy sigh, Deborah leaned back into the plush cushions of her sofa, her mind reeling with the events of the day. The meeting with Barak had left her feeling both encouraged and apprehensive, the magnitude of the task ahead looming large in her thoughts. She knew that taking on the conglomerate would be no small feat, that it would require every ounce of her strength, her wisdom, and her faith.

As the last rays of daylight faded from the sky,

Deborah closed her eyes, seeking solace in the quiet sanctuary of her own mind. And it was there, in the depths of her consciousness, that she felt it—a gentle but insistent tug, a whisper of divine guidance that seemed to emanate from the very core of her being.

Trust in me, the voice seemed to say, a soothing balm to her troubled spirit. *I have called you to this purpose, and I will be with you every step of the way.*

Deborah's eyes fluttered open, a single tear tracing a path down her cheek. She knew, with a certainty that defied explanation, that this was her calling, her destiny. That she had been chosen to lead this fight, to be a champion for the oppressed and a voice for the voiceless.

Rising to her feet, Deborah moved to stand before the window, her gaze fixed on the city below. The road ahead would be fraught with challenges, with obstacles that would test her resolve and her faith. But she knew, with a fierce and unwavering conviction, that she was ready to face whatever lay ahead.

For she was Deborah Lawson, a woman of strength, of wisdom, and of unyielding integrity. And with God as her guide and her shield, she would not rest until justice was served and the city she loved was free from the grip of corruption and greed.

CHAPTER 3

The flickering candlelight cast an amber glow across the anxious faces gathered in the cramped basement. Deborah stood at the head of the makeshift table, her piercing blue eyes surveying the eclectic group - community leaders, activists, legal experts - all united by a shared purpose. She cleared her throat, the sound cutting through the tense silence.

"Friends, we stand at a crossroads," Deborah began, her voice a beacon in the shadowy room. "The conglomerate's corruption threatens to engulf our city, to smother the very soul of our community. But together, we have the power to expose their misdeeds and restore justice."

Murmurs of agreement rippled through the gathering as Deborah leaned forward, her hands pressed against the scarred wooden surface. "We must be strategic, yet bold. Cautious, yet unrelenting. Each of you brings unique skills and influence to this fight. Together, we will weave a net of truth that even the conglomerate cannot escape."

As the group discussed potential strategies in hushed tones, Deborah's mind drifted to Barak. His hesitance, his self-doubt—they were luxuries they could no longer afford. She excused herself, slipping through the narrow stairwell and into the cool night air.

Barak's office was dimly lit, the weight of his responsibility evident in the slouch of his shoulders. Deborah entered, her presence filling the room with a palpable energy. "Barak," she said softly, "I know you're afraid. But fear is the conglomerate's most potent weapon. If we don't act now, their corruption will only spread, like a cancer eating away at the heart of our city."

He looked up at her, his brown eyes filled with a mix of trepidation and resignation. "I don't know if I'm strong enough, Deborah. What if I fail?"

She placed a hand on his shoulder, her touch a silent promise. "You won't face this alone. I will stand by you, every step of the way. Together, we will find the strength to do what must be done."

As Barak met her gaze, he felt a flicker of resolve ignite within him, a tiny flame against the darkness. Perhaps, with Deborah's unwavering support, he could find the courage to lead this fight. To become the leader their city so desperately needed.

The night stretched on, the secret meeting adjourning with a sense of shared purpose. Deborah walked the quiet streets, her mind turning over the challenges ahead. The path before them was treacherous, the odds daunting. But in the stillness of the night, she felt a glimmer of hope—a hope that, together, they could weave a tapestry of change, one thread at a time.

Barak stood before the assembled group, his hands clasped tightly behind his back. The weight of their collective gaze pressed upon him, a tangible force that made his heart race and his palms sweat. He glanced at Deborah, seeking reassurance in her steady presence. She nodded almost imperceptibly, a silent affirmation of her faith in him.

He took a deep breath, the air heavy with anticipation. "We have gathered evidence," he began, his voice barely above a whisper. He cleared his throat, willing himself to speak with more conviction. "Evidence that will expose the conglomerate's illicit activities and bring them to justice."

The room erupted in a chorus of murmurs, a mix of excitement and apprehension. Barak held up a hand, and the group fell silent once more. "But we must be strategic in our approach. We cannot afford to tip our hand too soon, lest they bury the truth and escape the consequences of their actions."

Deborah stepped forward, her voice clear and unwavering. "We propose a two-pronged approach. First, we will use investigative journalism to uncover the depth of their corruption and bring it to light. Second, we will pursue legal action, building an airtight case that will stand up in court."

As she spoke, Barak felt a surge of admiration for her strength and clarity of purpose. She was a beacon in the darkness, a guiding light that gave him the courage to press on.

The group erupted in a flurry of questions and suggestions, each member eager to contribute to the plan. Barak listened intently, his mind racing as he considered the challenges that lay ahead.

Could he truly lead this charge? Did he have the strength and the wisdom to see it through?

As if sensing his doubts, Deborah turned to him, her blue eyes locking with his. "Barak, we need you to be the public face of this effort. Your position and your reputation give you a platform that none of us can match."

He swallowed hard, the weight of her words settling upon his shoulders like a mantle. "I don't know if I'm ready," he whispered, his voice trembling.

She placed a hand on his arm, her touch a gentle reminder of her support. "You are ready. And you won't be alone. I will be with you, every step of the way."

In that moment, Barak felt a flicker of hope, a tiny spark that burned against the darkness. With Deborah by his side, perhaps he could find the strength to lead this fight. To become the leader their city so desperately needed.

As the meeting adjourned, Barak stood tall, his shoulders squared and his head held high. The road ahead was long and fraught with peril, but for the first time, he believed that they could prevail. That together, they could weave a tapestry of change, one thread at a time.

CHAPTER 4

Deborah peered at the newspaper splayed across her desk, its black and white pages proclaiming a truth she had long suspected. The bold headline glared up at her: *Conglomerate's Corrupt Dealings Exposed.* She felt a flicker of triumph amid the storm of emotions swirling inside.

The article, penned by a tenacious team of investigative journalists, laid bare the illegal partnerships and backroom deals that had allowed the conglomerate to tighten its grip on the city. With meticulous detail, the reporters unveiled a web of deceit that ensnared local politicians, implicating them in a scheme driven by greed and a lust for power.

Deborah's eyes scanned the names, some

familiar, others surprising in their complicity. She thought of the countless lives affected by these machinations—families struggling to make ends meet, small businesses suffocated by the conglomerate's unfair practices, dreams deferred and hopes extinguished. A righteous anger kindled within her, tempered by a steely resolve.

She reached for her phone, her fingers swift and purposeful as she dialed a number etched in her memory. Barak's voice, hesitant yet tinged with anticipation, greeted her on the second ring.

"Barak," Deborah said, her tone measured but urgent. "Have you seen the news?"

A pause, heavy with unspoken understanding. "I have." Barak's reply was soft, almost a whisper. "It's...it's overwhelming."

"But not unexpected," Deborah countered gently. She could sense Barak's inner turmoil, the weight of responsibility warring with his innate caution. "This is the evidence we've been waiting for. The truth we've known all along."

"What do we do now?" Barak asked, his question laden with uncertainty and a desperate need for guidance.

Deborah leaned back in her chair, her gaze drifting to the window that overlooked the city skyline. The towering skyscrapers, once symbols of progress and prosperity, now seemed to loom like sentinels of a corrupt regime. She knew the path forward would be fraught with challenges, but the alternative—a city suffocated by the conglomerate's unyielding grip—was unthinkable.

"We rally the people," Deborah said, her voice clear and unwavering. "We stand together and demand change. The truth is out there now, Barak. The people will not stand idly by."

A heavy silence followed, broken only by the distant sounds of the city awakening to the scandal. Barak's breathing, slightly uneven, crackled through the phone line. Deborah could sense his mind churning, grappling with the magnitude of the task before them.

"A rally," Barak finally said, his voice gaining strength. "At City Hall. We'll show the conglomerate that the people won't be silenced."

Deborah smiled, a flicker of pride igniting in her chest. Barak's words, though still tinged with apprehension, held a newfound determination. She knew that together, they could inspire a movement that would shake the very foundations of the city.

"I'll reach out to my contacts," Deborah said,

her mind already racing with plans. "We'll need to mobilize quickly, before the conglomerate has a chance to spin the story in their favor."

"I'll do the same," Barak replied, his tone resolute. "The people need to see their leaders united in this fight."

As the call ended, Deborah felt a surge of energy coursing through her veins. The road ahead would be long and arduous, but the wheels of change were already in motion. She glanced at the framed photograph on her desk, a snapshot of her younger self standing proudly beside her father. His words, spoken so long ago, echoed in her mind: "Stand firm in the face of adversity, Deborah. Fight for what is right, no matter the cost."

With renewed purpose, Deborah rose from her chair and strode towards the door. The battle for the soul of the city had begun, and she would be at the forefront, a beacon of hope in the darkness.

CHAPTER 5

Barak sat slumped in his office chair, the TV screen casting flickering shadows across his weary face. Headlines scrolled relentlessly, each one a vicious barb.

Deborah Lawson: Corrupt Crusader or Corporate Con Artist?

Exposé Reveals Shady Dealings of Lawson and Thompson

He felt like he was drowning, suffocating under the weight of the lies, the insinuations. All carefully crafted by that monster at Geracorps, no doubt. Jakob Anderton, the ruthless CEO who saw the world as pawns on a chessboard, to be manipulated and sacrificed at will. Barak shuddered, imagining those cold eyes and that mirthless shark smile.

A photo flashed on screen—him and Deborah, their integrity distorted through the lens of Anderton's smear campaign. Barak's stomach churned, bile rising in his throat. This was all so...dirty. He had wanted to make a difference, to stand up for what was right. But now...

His phone buzzed incessantly, no doubt more reporters hungry for a quote, ready to twist his words. He glanced at it, saw his wife's name. He couldn't face her, not now, not when doubt gnawed at his mind like a starving rat.

Was it worth it? Pursuing this mad crusade against a Goliath of money and power? Staking his reputation, his career, his family's stability on this precarious ledge of ideals?

Barak's shoulders slumped further, the weight of the world pressing down. Maybe he should just...stop. Step back before it was too late. Let someone else carry this burden, this searing scrutiny. He was just a man, flawed and fragile. Not some hero from a storybook.

He reached for the remote, thumb poised to banish the poison pouring from the screen. But he hesitated, transfixed by an image of Deborah at a podium, her eyes blazing with righteous fire even as the newscaster cut her down. That strength, that unshakable conviction. Could he turn his back on that?

Barak's hand trembled, caught between two worlds, two versions of himself. The one who stood tall no matter the cost...and the one who slunk away, tail between his legs.

The phone buzzed again, insistent, unrelenting. Like the choice before him. To crumble or to fight.

His thumb hovered, uncertain. The screen went black, his shadowy reflection staring back. Mocking. Waiting.

A gentle knock at the door startled Barak from his brooding reverie. He turned, hastily composing his features into a semblance of calm as Deborah entered, her presence filling the room like a warm glow.

She took in his haggard appearance, the deep circles under his eyes, the tightness in his jaw. Her gaze softened with understanding. "Rough day?"

Barak let out a humorless chuckle. "You could say that." He gestured vaguely at the dark television screen. "They're not pulling any punches."

Deborah settled into the chair beside him, her

movements graceful and purposeful. "They're scared, Barak. Scared of the truth we're bringing to light. Scared of losing their grip on power."

He sighed heavily, the weight of his doubts pressing down on his chest. "Maybe...maybe we're in over our heads here, Deborah. I mean, look at what they're doing to us. To our reputations. Our lives."

She leaned forward, capturing his gaze with her own. "I know it's hard. Believe me, I've had my own moments of doubt. But we can't let them win. Not when so much is at stake."

Barak shook his head, his voice barely above a whisper. "I don't know if I have the strength to keep fighting."

Deborah reached out, clasping his hand in her own. Her touch was warm, steadying. "You do, Barak. I've seen it. The way you stand up for what's right, even when it's not easy. The way you care about the people we're fighting for."

He met her eyes, seeing the unwavering faith shining there. Faith in him. In their cause. "What if it's not enough?"

She smiled then, a soft, knowing curve of her lips. "It is. Every day we keep going, every truth we uncover, every person we inspire to join us...it all matters. We're making a difference, Barak. Slowly but surely, we're changing things for the better."

Her words washed over him, easing the tightness in his chest. The doubts still lingered, but they seemed smaller now. More manageable.

Deborah squeezed his hand once more before releasing it. "We're in this together. Remember that. You're not alone."

Barak nodded, a faint smile tugging at the corners of his mouth. "Thank you, Deborah. For...for everything."

She rose to her feet, smoothing her skirt. "Anytime. Now, let's get back to work. We've got a lot to do."

As she headed for the door, Barak felt a renewed sense of purpose settling over him. The path ahead was still daunting, still fraught with obstacles and opposition. But with Deborah by his side, with the rightness of their cause to guide them...maybe, just maybe, they could see this through.

He stood, squaring his shoulders. Ready to face whatever came next. Together.

CHAPTER 6

The courtroom fell silent as Deborah rose from her seat, a pillar of unwavering resolve amidst the sea of spectators. She approached the podium with measured steps, her elegant suit a polished armor against the conglomerate's impending attacks. The cameras flashed, immortalizing the moment—David against Goliath, one woman's quest for justice against a behemoth of corporate greed.

Deborah's eyes met those of the judge, a silent acknowledgment passing between them. She took a deep breath, the weight of the city's future resting upon her shoulders. With a nod to her legal team, she began her opening statement, her voice clear and strong, reverberating through the hallowed halls of justice.

"Your Honor, esteemed members of the jury, we stand here today not just for ourselves, but for the very soul of our city." Deborah's words hung in the air, a palpable presence that demanded attention. "The evidence we shall present will unequivocally prove that the defendant, AweTech Conglomerate, has engaged in a pattern of corruption, exploitation, and blatant disregard for the well-being of our community."

As Deborah's team methodically laid out their case, presenting documents, witness testimonies, and damning audio recordings, the courtroom buzzed with a mixture of shock and outrage. The veneer of corporate respectability was stripped away, revealing the rotten core beneath. Deborah watched the faces of the jury, gauging their reactions, her heart swelling with each flicker of understanding in their eyes.

In the midst of the proceedings, a note was discreetly passed to Deborah. She unfolded it, her brow furrowing as she read the contents. It was from the conglomerate's CEO, requesting a private meeting during the recess. Deborah's gut twisted, instinctively sensing a trap. But curiosity and a desire to look her adversary in the eye propelled her forward.

The CEO greeted her with a shark's smile, all teeth and no warmth. "Ms. Lawson, let's dispense with the theatrics," he said, his voice dripping with condescension. "We both know this trial is a farce. But I'm willing to make you an offer—a generous settlement, and all of this goes away. You can be the hero, the savior of your precious city."

Deborah met his gaze unflinchingly, her voice steeled with conviction. "I'm not interested in your blood money," she replied, each word a dagger. "This isn't about me being a hero. It's about doing what's right, about ensuring that justice prevails. You may think you can buy your way out of anything, but not this time. Not on my watch."

With that, Deborah turned on her heel and strode away, leaving the CEO slack-jawed and seething. As she rejoined her team, a sense of calm descended upon her. They had truth on their side, and no amount of corporate posturing could change that. The battle was far from over, but in that moment, Deborah knew they would emerge victorious. For the city, for justice, and for the generations to come.

Barak stepped up to the podium, his heart pounding in his chest as he faced the sea of reporters and flashing cameras. The weight of the moment settled on his shoulders, and he gripped the sides of the lectern, his knuckles turning white. He took a deep breath, the words he had rehearsed tumbling through his mind in a jumble of uncertainty and self-doubt.

"Good afternoon," he began, his voice wavering slightly before finding its strength. "I stand before you today not just as an elected official, but as a citizen of this great city. A city that has been wronged, a city that deserves better."

The crowd hung on his every word, and Barak felt a flicker of confidence ignite within him. "The conglomerate thought they could silence us, thought they could buy our compliance with a settlement offer. But they underestimated the resolve of our people, the unbreakable spirit of this community."

Murmurs of agreement rippled through the audience, and Barak's voice grew stronger, more assured. "We will not be bought. We will not be cowed. We will stand firm in our pursuit of justice, no matter the cost. This is not just a legal battle—it is a moral imperative, a fight for the very soul of our city."

As he spoke, Barak felt a transformation taking place within himself. The hesitation that had always plagued him melted away, replaced by a newfound sense of purpose and conviction. He looked out at the faces of the people he served, saw the hope and determination in their eyes, and knew that he could not let them down.

"I ask you now, not as your representative, but as your neighbor, your friend—stand with us. Stand with Deborah Lawson and her team as they continue this fight. Let your voices be heard, let your presence be felt. Together, we can show the conglomerate that the power of the people is a force to be reckoned with."

The crowd erupted in cheers and applause, and Barak felt a swell of emotion rising in his chest. As he stepped back from the podium, he caught Deborah's eye, saw the gratitude and respect shining there. In that moment, he knew that he had found his true calling, his purpose. And he would not rest until justice was served, until his city was free from the grip of corruption and greed.

The tide was turning, the balance of power shifting. And with the support of the people, Barak knew that anything was possible. They would fight, they would persevere, and in the end, they would triumph. For the city, for each other, and for the generations to come.

CHAPTER 7

As the gavel struck with a resounding crack, Deborah felt the weight of the moment settle upon her shoulders. Her piercing blue eyes welled with tears of relief and vindication as the judge proclaimed the conglomerate guilty on all charges—corruption, bribery, extortion, a laundry list of crimes that had plagued their city for far too long.

Around her, the courtroom erupted into a cacophony of cheers and applause from the gallery packed with supporters and media. Deborah remained still, her tall, poised frame radiating a quiet dignity even as her heart soared with triumph. This was more than a legal victory; it was a turning point, a line drawn in the sand declaring that their city would no longer tolerate the rot of corruption.

In the ensuing chaos, Deborah's gaze drifted to the defendants' table, where the once-mighty executives now sat deflated, their arrogance punctured by the inescapable truth of their misdeeds laid bare before the eyes of justice. She felt a twinge of pity for them, these men who had sold their integrity for profit and power. What a hollow existence it must be, she mused, to live without a moral compass, beholden only to the whims of greed.

As the courtroom began to clear, Deborah turned to her team, her voice steady despite the emotion threatening to overwhelm her. "We did it," she said simply, clasping the hands of those nearest to her. "This is a victory for everyone who believes in fairness, in doing what's right."

Her words hung in the air, a promise and a challenge. They had won the battle, yes, but the war was far from over. Even now, Deborah knew that the conglomerate would not go quietly, that they would fight tooth and nail to maintain their hold on the city. But as she looked around at the faces of her allies, their eyes shining with renewed hope and determination, she felt a swell of certainty that they would prevail. Together, they would rebuild their city on a foundation of justice and integrity.

In the days that followed, the conglomerate began to crumble, its once-impenetrable facade cracking under the weight of public outrage and further investigations spurred by the court's ruling. One by one, its leaders fell from their lofty perches, disgraced and facing the consequences of their actions.

Amid the upheaval, a new generation of leaders emerged, men and women who shared Deborah's unwavering commitment to ethics and transparency. They stepped into the void left by the conglomerate's collapse, their voices ringing out with promises of reform and renewal.

As she watched this new era dawn, Deborah felt a sense of profound gratitude and humility. She had played her part, had fought the good fight, but she knew that this victory belonged to all of them—to every citizen who had stood up and said "enough," to every whistleblower who had risked everything to expose the truth, to every ally who had joined their cause.

There was still much work to be done, Deborah knew. The scars left by the conglomerate's misdeeds would not heal overnight. But as she looked out over her city, its streets pulsing with a newfound energy and purpose, she felt a flicker of something that had long been absent: hope. A hope for a future built on integrity, compassion, and the unshakable belief that together, they could forge a better world.

The grand hall buzzed with an electric energy as Deborah stepped up to the podium, the sea of faces before her a tapestry of joy, relief, and unbridled hope. She paused for a moment, her piercing blue eyes scanning the crowd, taking in the faces of those who had fought beside her, who had believed in the cause even when the odds seemed insurmountable.

Barak stood off to the side, his posture a little straighter, his eyes a little brighter. The journey had changed him, Deborah reflected. The hesitant, self-doubting man who had first joined their crusade had given way to someone more resolute, more sure of his convictions.

As the applause died down, Deborah began to speak, her voice ringing out clear and strong.

"Today, we stand here not just as victors, but as witnesses to the power of truth, the strength of unity, and the unbreakable spirit of our city."

Her words washed over the assembled crowd, each syllable imbued with the passion and conviction that had fueled their long fight. She spoke of the challenges they had faced, the setbacks they had endured, and the courage of those who had risked everything to bring the conglomerate's misdeeds to light.

"But this victory," Deborah continued, her voice softening, "is not mine alone. It belongs to each and every one of you. To the brave souls who stood up and spoke out, even when it meant putting your livelihoods, your reputations, and your safety on the line."

As she spoke, Deborah's mind drifted to the countless moments of doubt and uncertainty, the sleepless nights spent pouring over legal documents and strategizing with her team. It had been a long, grueling journey, one that had tested her resolve and her faith in the inherent goodness of people.

But standing here now, bathed in the warm glow of victory and surrounded by the faces of those who had fought alongside her, Deborah felt a sense of profound peace. They had done something remarkable, something that would echo through the annals of their city's history.

"Let this moment be a reminder," she said, her voice ringing with quiet intensity, "that no matter how daunting the challenge, no matter how powerful the opposition, the light of truth and justice will always prevail."

As the crowd erupted into cheers, Deborah stepped back from the podium, her heart full to bursting. Barak caught her eye from across the stage, a small smile playing at the corners of his mouth. In that moment, a silent understanding passed between them—a recognition of all they had been through, and all that was still to come.

For this was not the end of their journey, Deborah knew. It was merely the beginning. There would be more battles to fight, more wrongs to right. But armed with the knowledge of what they had achieved here today, she felt more ready than ever to face whatever lay ahead.

With a final wave to the crowd, Deborah descended from the stage, ready to embrace the future that stretched out before them—a future bright with promise and possibility.

EPILOGUE

The morning sun cast an amber glow over the city's skyline, its rays reflecting off the glass facades of newly erected buildings. Deborah gazed out the window of her corner office, a sense of pride swelling within her as she surveyed the fruits of their labors. The scars of corruption were fading, replaced by the budding promise of a brighter future.

A soft knock at the door drew her attention away from the panoramic view. "Come in," she called, her voice carrying the warmth of a mentor.

The door opened, revealing a young woman whose presence seemed to fill the room with an eager energy. Deborah recognized the fire in her eyes, a mirror of her own unyielding determination.

"Samantha, it's good to see you," Deborah said, gesturing for her to take a seat. "How are things progressing with the new initiative?"

The young woman sat down, her posture straight and confident. "We're making great strides, thanks to your guidance." She paused, a flicker of uncertainty crossing her features. "But I must admit, the responsibility can feel overwhelming at times."

Deborah leaned forward, her gaze softening with understanding. "I know that feeling all too well." She reached out, placing a reassuring hand on Samantha's arm. "Leadership is not about being perfect. I's about having the courage to make difficult decisions and the wisdom to learn from our mistakes."

Samantha nodded, absorbing the words like a sponge. "How do you maintain your integrity in the face of so much adversity?"

A wistful smile tugged at the corners of Deborah's mouth. "It's a constant battle," she admitted. "But I find strength in remembering why we do this work." She gestured towards the city sprawling before them. "We fight for those who cannot fight for themselves, to create a world where justice and compassion reign."

As the two women continued their conversation, the sun climbed higher in the sky, illuminating the path ahead. Deborah knew that the journey was far from over, but with each passing day, the city inched closer to the ideals they held dear. And in Samantha, she saw the promise of a new generation, ready to take up the mantle and lead with unwavering integrity.

Deborah's mind drifted back to the early days of her crusade, when the city was mired in corruption and despair. The memory of those dark times still haunted her, a constant reminder of how far they had come and how much work lay ahead. Yet, amidst the challenges, there had been moments of profound triumph—the day she exposed the truth about her corrupt predecessor, the groundswell of support from the community, and the first tangible signs of change.

As she gazed out over the city, Deborah couldn't help but feel a sense of awe at the transformation that had taken place. The once-dilapidated buildings now stood tall and proud, their facades gleaming in the sunlight. The streets, once littered with debris and despair, now buzzed with the energy of a populace filled with renewed hope. It was a testament to the resilience of the human spirit and the power of collective action.

Deborah's thoughts turned to the future, and a sense of peace washed over her. She knew that the fight for justice was an eternal one, that there would always be those who sought to exploit and oppress. But she also knew that as long as there were people like Samantha—passionate, principled, and determined—the city would never again succumb to the darkness.

With a deep breath, Deborah turned to her young protégé, a fire burning in her eyes. "Never forget, Samantha, that our strength lies not in our individual abilities, but in the unity of our purpose. Together, we can weather any storm and overcome any obstacle."

Samantha met her gaze, a fierce determination etched on her face. "I won't let you down, Deborah. I promise to carry on your legacy and fight for what is right, no matter the cost."

Deborah smiled, her heart swelling with pride and gratitude. She had no doubt that Samantha would be a force for good in the world, a beacon of hope for generations to come. And as she looked out over the city once more, she knew that her own journey had been worth every sacrifice, every struggle, every moment of doubt. For in the end, she had made a difference—and that was a legacy that would endure long after she was gone.

EXCERPT FROM LOST AND FOUND

Stuck in a maze
of confusion.
No ending in sight,
I cannot navigate
this corruption
on my own.
I fall to my knees
in despair.
I am unworthy
but please
find me.

— FIND ME

Lost and Found is a collection of spiritual poems that illustrate the journey from darkness to salvation.

Get Lost and Found: Poems to Take You From Darkness to Light now!

ABOUT THE AUTHOR

Award-winning author Kayla Lowe writes women's fiction that explores complex themes with sensitivity and depth. Kayla's books delve into the intricacies of relationships, self-discovery, and resilience. From cozy love stories interspersed with a bit of faith to heartwarming tales of friendship and suspenseful novels of empowerment and heartbreak, her books illustrate the struggles specific to women.

When she's not churning out her next novel, you can find her with her feet in the sand and a book in her hand or curled up on the couch with her dogs.

Visit her website at www.authorkaylalowe.com.

ALSO BY KAYLA LOWE

<u>Honeyed Kisses (Book 4)</u>

<u>Blooming Forever (Book 5)</u>

<u>Strawberry Beach Series</u>

<u>Beachside Lessons (Book 1)</u>

<u>Beachside Lessons (Book 2)</u>

<u>Beachside Lessons (Book 3)</u>

Panama City Beach Series

Sun-Kissed Secrets (Book 1)

Sun-Kissed Secrets (Book 2)

Sun-Kissed Secrets (Book 3)

The Tainted Love Saga

Of Love and Deception (Book 1)

Of Love and Family (Book 2)

Of Love and Violence (Book 3)

Of Love and Abuse(Book 4)

Of Love and Crime (Book 5)

Of Love and Addiction (Book 6)

Of Love and Redemption (Book 7)

<u>Standalones</u>

Maiden's Blush

<u>Poetry</u>

Phantom Poetry

Lost and Found